We all worry from time to time and that is normal. We also have different thoughts about what to do when we are worried. Sometimes we have two different thoughts about what to do. You can call these different thoughts Bubble and Slug.

Read on to see how some kids just like you deal with feeling worried and learn what happens when they choose which thoughts to embrace: Bubble or Slug. As you read, you will choose how each kid should handle each situation. Should they listen to Bubble or should they listen to Slug?

Hi! I'm Bubble!

Hi! I'm Slug!

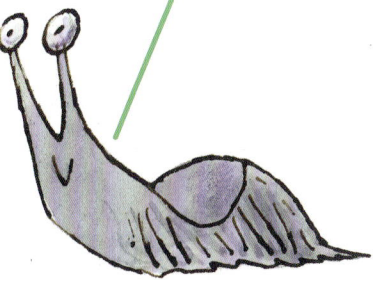

www.FlowerpotPress.com
DJS-0810-0200
ISBN: 978-1-4867-2117-7
Made in China. Fabriqué en Chine.

Copyright © 2021 Flowerpot Press,
a Division of Flowerpot Children's Press, Inc., Oakville, ON, Canada and Kamalu LLC, Franklin, TN, U.S.A. All rights reserved. Can you find the flowerpot? No part of this publication may be reproduced, stored in a retrieval system or transmitted, in any form or by any means, electronic, mechanical, photocopying, recording, optical scan, or otherwise, without the prior written permission of the copyright holder.

The Invitation

Sophia was excited to be invited to Maya's party! But the more she thought about it, the more she began to worry.

Sophia was definitely going to be the tallest kid at the birthday party. She was so worried about it that she began to think maybe she shouldn't go. Sophia thought the party would not be fun for her. That's when Bubble and Slug started talking...

Did Sophia listen to Bubble? Turn to page **10**.
Did Sophia listen to Slug? Turn to page **8**.

Slug told Sophia she was right.

"Being tall is the worst!" said Slug. "Playing the limbo game is WAY too hard! And other birthday games are so awkward when you're the tallest person there."

Sophia listened to Slug and decided not to go to the party. She would just wait a couple years and hope her friends would grow taller so she would not feel like such an odd duck. That night at dinner, while talking to her parents, she didn't have any fun stories to share. She had spent the whole day at home feeling bored.

Bubble told Sophia she should take a chance and go to the party.

"Being tall is the best!" said Bubble. "Whacking piñatas is easy when you're tall! Sure, some of the games aren't as easy, but they're still a lot of fun."

Sophia listened to Bubble and decided she would rather jump in and have fun than stay at home and worry. That night at dinner, Sophia talked nonstop about all the fun she had at the party. She was happy she had taken a chance.

A Stormy Night

Lucas didn't like storms. He REALLY didn't like storms. Lucas had trouble falling asleep on stormy nights. He listened to the thunder and stared out at the lightning and thought nothing good could come from all that flashing and noise. Lucas worried that if he fell asleep something bad would happen. That's when Bubble and Slug started talking...

Did Lucas listen to Bubble? Turn to page **16**.
Did Lucas listen to Slug? Turn to page **14**.

Slug told Lucas he was right.

"Storms are scary," said Slug. "If you don't keep an eye on this one, there is no telling what could go wrong!"

So Lucas stayed awake feeling scared and worried for hours. The next morning, when Lucas had to get up for school, he was exhausted.

Bubble told Lucas he was right.

"Storms are scary, but only if you want them to be," said Bubble. "They can also be great if you want them to be. Try thinking about storms in a different way!"

Bubble told Lucas that rather than focusing on the bad things about storms, he should make a list of all the songs he knows with storm words in them, like "Rain, Rain, Go Away" and "Singin' in the Rain."

Lucas stopped worrying about the storm and started thinking about all the songs he knew. As he started singing one in his head, he began to drift off to sleep. The next morning he woke up feeling great!

The School Bullies

Jackson was having a really hard time with two kids in his class. Ava would shove him every time he was walking to lunch and her twin brother, Aiden, would always laugh and spill something on Jackson as he fell. After the third time this happened, Jackson was fed up. But he was worried nothing would ever make them stop. That's when Bubble and Slug started talking...

Did Jackson listen to Bubble? Turn to page **22**.
Did Jackson listen to Slug? Turn to page **20**.

Slug told Jackson it was time to get even.

"Fight fire with fire!" shouted Slug.

Jackson stood up with both hands full of pudding and threw it all over Ava and Aiden. Then he ran at them swinging his arms. The lunch monitor stopped the three kids and took them to the principal's office. All three of them were in big trouble. Now Jackson is worried he made the situation worse and the twins will just start picking on him again tomorrow.

Bubble told Jackson he was right.

"Enough is enough. Let's put an end to this," said Bubble.

That sounded like a good idea to Jackson, so he talked to the lunch monitor about what was going on. She listened to Jackson and got the principal involved. The principal sat down with all three kids and helped them work it out. Now Jackson and the twins are slowly becoming friends.

The New Kid

School started three days ago and Isabella still had not made any new friends. She was watching the kids play soccer and thinking about how much she would love to play. But Isabella worried that nobody would like it if she joined in without being asked. That's when Bubble and Slug started talking...

Did Isabella listen to Bubble? Turn to page **28**.
Did Isabella listen to Slug? Turn to page **26**.

Slug told Isabella she was right.

"You don't know these kids and they didn't ask you to play with them, so you better stay away," said Slug.

Isabella sat on the side of the field. She spent all of recess wishing she was playing soccer. As she went back inside after recess, Isabella worried she would never get to play.

Bubble told Isabella she could do this!

"Strangers are just friends you haven't met yet!" said Bubble.

Isabella went to the side of the field and took five big breaths. As she breathed in, she squeezed her hands together and thought about all the positive energy the world was sending in through her nose. As she breathed out, she relaxed her hands and thought about the negative energy she was sending out through her mouth. Charged full of excitement and ready to go, Isabella ran onto the field and asked if she could play. All the kids were excited that Isabella wanted to play, and they were looking forward to getting to know her better. As Isabella went back inside after recess, she thought to herself, I cannot wait until tomorrow to play again!

Worry is a normal emotion that we all feel from time to time. Whether you are reading this book by yourself or if you are a parent or friend reading it with someone else, I hope this book helps you see some of the ways you can deal with the things that make you worry. Everyone can have a Bubble and Slug on their shoulder and the one we listen to can have a big impact on our day.

Think about the adventures in this book. How did they make you feel? Read the discussion questions below and try answering each one out loud with a teacher, parent, or friend.

THE INVITATION

Did you pick Slug or Bubble? Why?
Were you happy with your decision? Why or why not?

When you found out Sophia felt unwelcome due to her height, how did that make you feel?

How did you feel when Sophia listened to Bubble and had a great time with all of her friends? Did it remind you of any birthday parties you've been to?

How did you feel when Sophia listened to Slug and decided not to go to the party? Have you ever decided not to go somewhere because you were afraid you wouldn't be welcome?

Have you ever felt like you didn't fit in because of the way you look? How did that make you feel?

Can you think of something about your appearance that makes you feel unique or special?

A STORMY NIGHT

Did you pick Slug or Bubble? Why? Were you happy with your decision? Why or why not?

When Lucas said he was afraid of the thunder and lightning, how did it make you feel?

Have you ever had trouble sleeping because of a storm? Is there anything else that has made you worry during the night?

How did Bubble's thoughts about storms make you feel? Did it help you think about things that are scary in a new light?

How did you feel after Slug gave Lucas advice? How did you feel when Lucas wasn't able to sleep and had to go to school the next day?

Have you been scared of storms in the past? If so, how were you able to overcome that fear? If not, what's your favorite part about storms?

THE SCHOOL BULLIES

Did you pick Slug or Bubble? Why? Were you happy with your decision? Why or why not?

How did you feel when Ava shoved Jackson and Aiden spilled water on him?

How did you feel when Jackson listened to Bubble and talked to his principal about his problem? Did it remind you of a time when you had to tell an adult about a problem you were having?

How did you feel when Jackson got in trouble after listening to Slug? Have you ever gotten in trouble for something you thought was a good idea when it actually wasn't?

Have you ever had to deal with a school bully? How did you handle the situation?

Was there ever somebody you didn't like very much when you first met them but you eventually became friends?

THE NEW KID

Did you pick Slug or Bubble? Why? Were you happy with your decision? Why or why not?

How did you feel when Isabella hadn't made any friends after being at school for three days? Have you ever had trouble making friends?

How did you feel when Isabella listened to Bubble and was able to make new friends? Did it remind you of a time when you made new friends?

How did you feel when Isabella sat away from everyone else after she listened to advice from Slug? Did it remind you of a time when you had to sit alone?

Have you ever been afraid of making friends?

Were you ever the new kid at school? How did you make friends? If not, did you ever try to welcome kids who were new at your school?

The Which Ugly Fruit Am I? Chart

I created this emotion chart because I think the Jamaican tangelo is a great example for all of us. The Jamaican tangelo is a delicious fruit—fantastic on the inside but a little out of the ordinary on the outside. This fruit chose to embrace its uniqueness and is now most often referred to as the Ugly Fruit. It had fun embracing its differences and since then has become much more popular. I like to think that much like the Jamaican tangelo, we can all achieve greater success by learning to embrace what makes us unique and celebrate it.

As you read the adventures in this book, use this chart to help you think about which emotion shows how you would feel before and after each situation.

Do you notice a pattern? Try reading this book by skipping the Slug thinking and picking the Bubble thinking each time. I think you might like how it makes you feel.

Gail Hayes, M.A.

HAPPY   **GRATEFUL**

CALM   **FRUSTRATED**

JEALOUS   **CONCERNED**   **JOYFUL**

  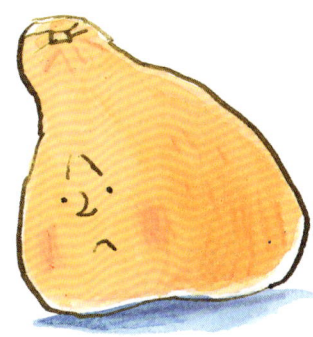

FEARFUL   **PROUD**   **LONELY**

EXCITED   **SAD**   **WORRIED**

LOVED   **DISAPPOINTED**   **SAFE**